1/09

The Little Runaway

DEAR CAREGIVER, The *Beginning-to-Read* series is a carefully written collection of classic readers you may remember from your own childhood. Each book features text comprised of common sight words to provide your child ample practice reading the words that appear most frequently in written text. The many additional details in the pictures enhance the story and offer the opportunity for you to help your child expand oral language and develop comprehension.

Begin by reading the story to your child, followed by letting him or her read familiar words and soon your child will be able to read the story independently. At each step of the way, be sure to praise your reader's efforts to build his or her confidence as an independent reader. Discuss the pictures and encourage your child to make connections between the story and his or her own life. At the end of the story, you will find reading activities and a word list that will help your child practice and strengthen beginning reading skills.

Above all, the most important part of the reading experience is to have fun and enjoy it!

Shannon Cannon

Shannon Cannon,
Literacy Consultant

Norwood House Press • P.O. Box 316598 • Chicago, Illinois 60631
For more information about Norwood House Press please visit our website at *www.norwoodhousepress.com* or call 866-565-2900.

LIBRARY OF CONGRESS CATALOGING-IN-PUBLICATION DATA
  Hillert, Margaret.
    The little runaway / Margaret Hillert ; illustrated by Irv Anderson. —
  Rev. and expanded library ed.
      p. cm. — (Beginning-to-read series)
    Summary: "Recounts the adventures of a runaway kitten"—Provided by
  publisher.
    ISBN-13: 978-1-59953-155-7 (library edition : alk. paper)
    ISBN-10: 1-59953-155-0 (library edition : alk. paper) [1. Cats—Fiction.
  2. Animals—Infancy—Fiction.] I. Anderson, Irv, ill. II. Title.
  PZ7.H558Li 2008
  [E]—dc22   2007035629

Beginning-to-Read series (c) 2009 by Margaret Hillert.
Library edition published by permission of Pearson Education, Inc. in
arrangement with Norwood House Press, Inc. All rights reserved.
This book was originally published by Follett Publishing Company in 1966.

The Little Runaway

by Margaret Hillert
Illustrated by Irv Anderson

Here is a mother.
Here is a little baby.

Come here, little one.
Come here to me.

No, no.
I want to go away.
Here I go.
One, two, three.

Away, away.
It is fun to run away.
Away I go.

I can run.
I can jump.
I can play.

Look up, look up.
Something is up.

Something can go away.
See it go away.
Away, away, away.

I see something.
Something red.
Something yellow.

Down, down, down.
See something come down.
It is fun to play here.

Look up, up, up.
See the little balls.
Little and red.

Oh, oh, oh.
Oh, my.
Oh, my.
It is not funny.

Here is something blue.
I can look down in it.

Help, help!

Oh, oh.
I want to go away.

Work, work, work.
You can work.
I see you work.

21

Come and play.
We can play.

Up, up, up.
I can not go up.

Oh my, oh my.
Something big.
Big, big, big.

Oh, oh, oh.
Where is my mother?
Help, help.

Mother, Mother, I want you.
I want my mother.
It is not fun to run away.

Here, little one.
Here is Mother.
Come to Mother.

WORD LIST

The Little Runaway uses the 45 words listed below.
This list can be used to practice reading the words that appear in the text.
You may wish to write the words on index cards and use them to help your
child build automatic word recognition. Regular practice with these words
will enhance your child's fluency in reading connected text.

a	help	oh	want
and	here	one	we
away			where
	I	play	work
baby	in		
balls	is	red	yellow
big	it	run	you
blue			
	jump	see	
can		something	
come	little		
	look	the	
down		three	
	me	to	
fun	mother	two	
funny	my		
		up	
go	no		
	not		

ABOUT THE AUTHOR Margaret Hillert has written over 80 books for
children who are just learning to read. Her books
have been translated into many different languages and over a million children
throughout the world have read her books. She first started writing poetry as
a child and has continued to write for children and adults throughout her life. A
first grade teacher for 34 years, Margaret is now retired from teaching and lives in
Michigan where she likes to write, take walks in the morning, and care for her three cats.

Photograph by Glenna Washburn

ABOUT THE ADVISER Shannon Cannon contributed the activities pages that appear in
this book. Shannon serves as a literacy consultant and provides
staff development to help improve reading instruction. She is a frequent presenter at educational
conferences and workshops. Prior to this she worked as an elementary school teacher and as
president of a curriculum publishing company.